MICE ON ICE

by Jane Yolen

pictures by Lawrence Di Fiori

A Smart Cat Book

E. P. Dutton   New York

Library of Congress Cataloging in Publication Data

Yolen, Jane   Mice on ice.
(A Smart cat book)

SUMMARY: The famous inventor of an ice-making formula must rescue a skating star of the Mice Capades from kidnappers.
[1. Ice skating—Fiction.   2. Kidnapping—Fiction.
3. Mice—Fiction]   I. Di Fiori, Lawrence.   II. Title.
III. Series: Smart cat book.
PZ7.Y78Mf   [E]   79-19342   ISBN: 0-525-34872-7

Published in the United States by E. P. Dutton, a Division of Elsevier-Dutton Publishing Company, Inc., New York

Published simultaneously in Canada by Clarke, Irwin & Company Limited, Toronto and Vancouver

Editor: Ann Durell   Designer: Claire Counihan
Printed in the U.S.A.   First Edition
10 9 8 7 6 5 4 3 2 1

for the members of the

E. P. M. S. M. B. and C. E. C.

who heard it first

J. Y.

for Mother

L. D.

Contents

The Tent

In the middle of a grassy field was a tent. It had not been there the day before. But now flags flew from its top. In front of the tent was a big sign:

SHOW TODAY

A crowd stood in line to get in. Gypsy moths told their fortunes while they waited.

7

"Just one nut a ticket," called a mouse in a black hat. "Come in and see the Mice on Ice."

The crowd was happy. They laughed and talked as they went into the tent. When the last mouse had paid, it was time for the show.

The mouse in the black hat went in last. He closed the tent flap after him. His name was Horace Hopper. He owned the show.

Horace Hopper went into the middle of the tent. There was a large ring of water. It looked like a lake.

Horace made little waves.

Then Horace took a bottle from his
pocket. He held it up for the crowd
to see.

No one in the crowd said a word.
They hardly seemed to breathe.

Horace turned the bottle over. He
let two drops drip out. They splashed
into the lake. In an instant the water
had turned white and hard. It was ice.

"Yay!" called the crowd. "Yay, Horace!" For Horace was an inventor. He was famous all over the world.

Horace held up his paw. The crowd was silent again. "Ladies and gentlemen of West Cheddar," he said. "Mouselets of all ages. I now give you the star of our show. Miss Rosa Burrow-Minder. And with her—the Mice Skaters!"

The crowd cheered again.

A light came on. It pointed to a
hole at the top of the tent. Down
through that hole came a quarter
moon. It was made of green cheese.
On the moon sat Rosa Burrow-Minder.
The star.

Down and down and down came the moon. Miss Rosa smiled. Her skates touched the ice.

The band began to play.

From the sides of the tent skated nineteen other mice.

The Mice Capades had begun.

The Rat King

Meanwhile, something bad was about to happen.

A mile away there was a secret hideout under the ground. It had twenty connecting tunnels. It was owned by Gomer the Rat King. He was a mouse who had gone bad.

Gomer snarled. It was his special way of talking. "I'll get that Horace Hopper. I'll show him who is the most important rodent around here."

Gomer's four giant bodyguards
smiled. They were called the Four
Muscles. They did not have to be told
who was the most important mouse
around. They knew it was Gomer,
their boss. He was the Underworld's
Big Cheese.

"I'll catch that Horace Hopper in my trap!" said Gomer the Rat King.

"Yeh!" said the Four Muscles.

"Then snap!" said Gomer.

"SNAP! SNAP! SNAP! SNAP!" the Four Muscles said.

Gomer rubbed his paws together.
He smiled, and his yellow teeth shone.
"Then I will have the ice-making
formula. I will have Miss Rosa
Burrow-Minder. And that creep
Horace will have nothing."

"Yeh!" said the Four Muscles.

Gomer lay down on his sofa. "Now here is my plan," said Gomer.

"Yeh!" said the Four Muscles. They listened with their ears but not with their brains. It was all they really needed for Gomer's plan.

The Mice Capades

The band played a march by the well-known composer John Philip Mousa. The nineteen Mice Skaters flowed out on the ice.

They did loop-de-loops.

They did figure eights.

They did one-foot glides and flip-flops in the air.

The crowd cheered.

Then Miss Rosa Burrow-Minder began to skate. She moved like a feather in the wind.

Miss Rosa did loop-de-loop-de-loops.

She did figure eights, nines, tens, and twenty-fours. (That is three figure eights together.)

Her one-foot glides were held longer than anyone else's. And her flip-flops were like flying.

When she finished, the crowd stood up. They cheered and cheered and cheered.

Miss Rosa skated back to the green cheese moon and sat down on it.

Up and up and up and up went the
moon. Miss Rosa waved and smiled.
Up and up and up. She stopped smiling.

The moon did not stop. It kept
going. Higher and higher. Faster and
faster. It was out of control.

Gomer's Plan

All that was part of Gomer the Rat King's plan. He had put a large magnet into the green cheese moon.

When Rosa Burrow-Minder was pulled to the top of the tent, the gypsy moths were waiting. They were in Gomer the Rat King's pay. They carried a great big magnet.

Miss Rosa never had a chance. Up
and up and up she went. She noticed
nothing wrong until she was near the
top of the tent. By then it was too
late.

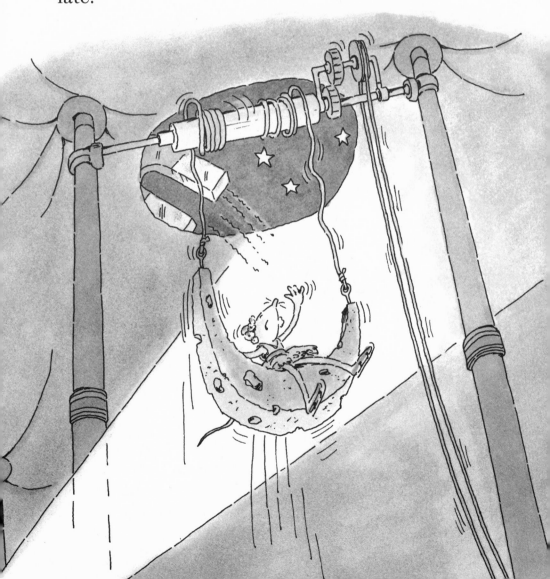

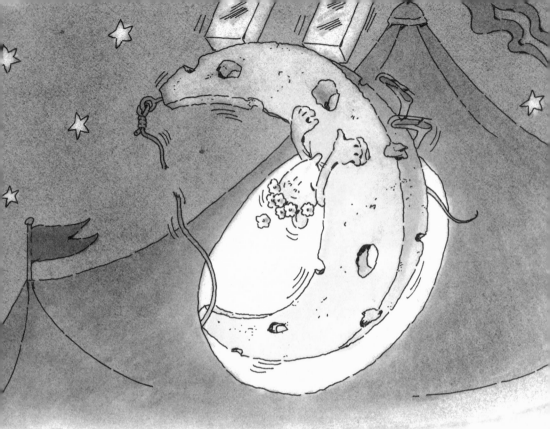

Up and up and up Miss Rosa went.
Up and out of the tent she went on
the green cheese moon.

TWANG.

SNAP.

The two magnets met. The gypsy
moths towed the green cheese away.
Miss Rosa clung to it, afraid.

As they went, the moths sang a
gypsy ransom song. It went something
like this:

> The Rat's got the cheese,
> The Rat's got the cheese,
> Hi-ho the dairy-o,
> The Rat's got the cheese...
>   and pretty Rosa.

The Missing Mouse

The skaters came back onto the ring of ice. Horace slid out with them.

Horace was worried. He was worried and scared and sick. He wrung his paws.

"What could have happened? Who could have done this?" He spoke to himself, but all the Mice Skaters heard him.

"What could have happened?" they said back. "Who could have done this?"

Just then a note sailed down from the top of the tent. Horace picked it up. He opened it.

DO YOU WANT TO SEE
MISS ROSA AGAIN?

1. Bring ice formula
2. Go to third old oak on
   Swiss Cheese Lane
3. Come at twelve
4. Come alone

   —Gomer the Rat King

"What can we do?" asked the Mice Skaters together.

Horace looked up from the note. "Do? Just what the note says to do."

"WHAT?" The Mice Skaters looked at one another. Then they all started talking at once. "Give away the ice formula? Gomer the Rat King would

use it for evil. He could rob banks and turn the walks to ice. The police would fall flat on their faces. Gomer would skate away free."

"Yes," said Horace. "I know all that. But still we will do what the note says. But . . ."

The skaters waited.

"But we will add something all our own," Horace said. "We are in luck. It is just starting to rain outside."

The skaters gathered around him. "Rain?" they asked. "What good is rain?"

"You will find out," said Horace. "First, I need a helper."

Every mouse raised a paw.

"A very small helper," said Horace.

"I'm the smallest." Up stepped little Ruby Burrow-Minder. She was Miss Rosa's baby sister.

"It could be dangerous. Are you sure?" asked Horace.

"I'm sure," said Ruby.

"Then," said Horace, "here is my plan."

Horace Follows the Note

The hours moved very slowly. Horace and little Ruby moved very fast.

When they left the tent, a light rain was falling. Horace drove his truck down Swiss Cheese Lane. He came to the third old oak.

"Ready?" Horace said to the back of the truck.

"Ready," said Ruby. She was dressed all in black. She had on a black cap and black gloves and black tights.

Horace parked the truck. He got out and waited under the tree.

A black shadow came out after him. It was Ruby. She hid behind the tree.

Horace began to whistle. It made
him feel brave. It also covered any
noises Ruby made.

There was a loud screech. A squeal
of wheels. A long, low car came to a
stop. Out jumped the Four Muscles.

"Do you have the ice formula?" they called.

"Yes," said Horace. "Do you have Miss Rosa?"

"Yes," they called back.

"You first," said Horace.

"No, you first," said the Four Muscles.

"Okay," said Horace, walking back to his truck. "It's over here."

The Four Muscles followed him. They had their backs to their own car.

The tiny black shadow left the tree. It tied something to the rear of the long, low car. Then it slipped back behind the tree.

"Here!" said Horace. He held out a bottle.

One of the Four Muscles grabbed the formula. They all laughed on the way back to their long, low car.

"Where is Miss Rosa?" called Horace.

"We may be dumb," said the Four Muscles. "But we are not THAT dumb."

They jumped into their car. It roared out of sight.

"Dumber!" said Ruby as she stepped from behind the tree.

Horace smiled. "They sure are," he said.

Mouse Power

Horace and Ruby got into the truck. They raced back to the tent. The Mice Skaters were waiting.

"Where is Miss Rosa?" they asked.

"They didn't bring her," said Horace. "Just as we thought."

Little Ruby spoke up. "We tied the formula bottle to their car."

"Then, let's go!" cried the Mice Skaters.

Each Mice Skater took a pail of water and a pair of skates. They climbed into the back of the truck.

They drove to the third old oak.
Rain was still falling. The formula tied
to the long, low car had dripped out
of the bottle. The road behind the car
had turned to ice.

The Mice Skaters got out of the
truck. Each one picked up a pail.
Then they skated down the ice road
and into the dark.

Even Horace put on a pair of skates.
He skated faster than all the others.

At last they came to a field. There
was the long, low car. And there was
a hole. It went into a tunnel.

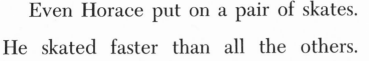

"I'll go first," said Horace. He dumped his pail of water down the hole. Then he poured some formula into the hole. In a second, an ice-way shone.

"Follow me," Horace called as he skated out of sight.

The Mice Skaters followed. There were no loop-de-loops or figure eights now. Just silent mouse power.

In less than an hour, the Mice Skaters had iced over nineteen tunnels and skated down every one.

The last four tunnels ended in a big
room. The Mice Skaters reached it at
the same time. They stopped and
looked in.

There was Gomer the Rat King on
his sofa. The Four Muscles stood next
to him, smiling.

Miss Rosa was tied in a chair.

The Big Fight

"Now!" called Horace.

The Mice Skaters leaped in through the tunnel openings.

At that, the Four Muscles turned. They were dumb, but they knew how to fight.

The Four Muscles threw off one, then two, then three Mice Skaters. They punched. They poked. They pounded.

"Water!" called Horace, who had run to Miss Rosa's side.

"Water!" Ruby called back. She lifted her pail. Splash!

Horace dripped formula onto the water. The floor turned to ice.

The Four Muscles were not used to
ice. They had no skates. They turned,
slipped, and fell down.

Before they could get up, the Mice Skaters piled on top of them.

Horace smiled. Then he turned to Miss Rosa and untied her paws.

"But where is Gomer the Rat King?" asked little Ruby. She pulled at Horace's coat.

Horace looked around. "Yes," he asked, "where is Gomer?"

Miss Rosa put her paw in the air. "Gone," she said. "That way."

They all looked up. There was a large pole. At the top of it was the sofa. It had lifted, like an elevator, and carried Gomer to the top of the room. There was a special get-away hole in the ceiling.

"I'll get him," called Horace. He shinnied up the pole. He climbed over the sofa and pulled himself up into the hole.

"Be careful!" called out Miss Rosa. Horace called back. "Time for paw-to-paw combat!" Then he disappeared.

Paw-to-Paw

The get-away hole led to a secret tunnel. It was the one tunnel that was not iced over. Horace had to take off his skates.

Horace was scared. He was scared but he was mad, too. So he did not stop. He ran and ran and ran down the tunnel. It came out behind a rock.

On the other side of the rock was
the long, low car. In it was Gomer the
Rat King.

"Stop!" called Horace.

Gomer just looked at him and laughed. He reached into his pocket for the key. Then he remembered. The Four Muscles still had the key. Gomer stopped laughing. He jumped out of the car and tried to run.

He slipped on the ice and fell.

Horace leaped a mighty leap. He landed on Gomer's back and bit Gomer's ear.

"Owowowowowowowow," cried Gomer and rolled over on his back in the wet grass.

"Owowowowowowowow," cried Horace. He let go of Gomer's ear. But he held on to Gomer's neck.

Gomer reached up over his head. He caught Horace's nose.

Just then little Ruby came out of another tunnel. "I'll help, Horace," she called.

She knew she was too small to hit Gomer. But she also knew she had to do something. She slid over to the long, low car. She untied the formula bottle from the rear. Then she ran over and sprinkled the last bit of formula on the two fighting mice.

They were wet from the light rain.
They were wet from the grass. In less
than a minute, they froze.

"At least that will slow them down
while I think this over," said little
Ruby.

After the Melt

Miss Rosa had called the police.
Just as the sun came up, they arrived.
They took the Four Muscles to jail.

64

The Mice Skaters put the ice statue
of Horace and Gomer into the truck,
and they drove after the police.

At the jail, the police made a big
fire. They put the ice statue near it.

The Mice Skaters stood in a circle and watched. Drip by drip by drop Horace and Gomer were freed.

First they could move their heads.

"Creep," said Gomer.

"Mouse-napper," said Horace.

Then they could move their arms.

But before they could hit each
other, the police held their paws. They
held them until the last drop had
dripped.

A sad song came from the cells. The gypsy moths had given themselves up. They said they were sorry. Miss Rosa and Horace forgave them. The Mice Skaters forgave them. All except little Ruby.

The police let the gypsy moths go. They flew off singing a gypsy freedom song.

But Gomer and the Four Muscles
stayed in jail. They would be there for
a long long time.

The policemen all went to the next
show of the Mice Capades.

Miss Rosa twirled and loop-de-
looped.

The Mice Skaters did figure eights
and even nines and tens.

Little Ruby got to wear the big black hat.

And they all skated happily ever after.